Anastasio, Dina.

Joy to the world!

$7.99

DATE			

JOY TO THE WORLD!
The Story of Christmas

A Platt & Munk **ALL ABOARD BOOK™**

 Published by Platt & Munk, Publishers, a division of Grosset & Dunlap, Inc., which is a member of The Putnam & Grosset Group, New York. ALL ABOARD BOOKS is a trademark of The Putnam & Grosset Group. THE LITTLE ENGINE THAT COULD and engine design are trademarks of Platt & Munk, Publishers. Published simultaneously in Canada. Printed in the U.S.A.

Library of Congress Cataloging-in-Publication Data
Anastasio, Dina. Joy to the world : the story of Christmas / retold by Dina Anastasio ; illustrated by Bettina Paterson. p. cm. — (All aboard books) Summary: Retells the story of the birth of Jesus Christ. 1. Jesus Christ—Nativity—Juvenile literature. [1. Jesus Christ—Nativity. 2. Bible stories—N.T.] I. Paterson, Bettina, ill. II. Title. III. Series.
BT315.2.A49 1992 232.92—dc20 91-44468 CIP AC
ISBN 0-448-40479-6 (paperback) A B C D E F G H I J
ISBN 0-448-40480-X (library) A B C D E F G H I J

JOY TO THE WORLD!
The Story of Christmas

Retold by Dina Anastasio
Illustrated by Bettina Paterson

Platt & Munk, Publishers

Long, long ago, in the town of Nazareth, there lived a woman whose name was Mary. One day an angel named Gabriel appeared to her and said, "Mary, you have been chosen by God to have a baby, a boy you will call Jesus. And he will be known as the Son of God."

The angel's words came to pass. Mary was going to have a baby. Not long before the baby was born, Mary and her husband Joseph traveled to the village of Bethlehem. Mary rode their donkey and Joseph walked alongside. It was a long, hard, slow trip, and when they arrived in the little town, Mary and Joseph were very tired.

They knocked on the door of the inn, but the innkeeper said there was no room for them.

So, they tied up the donkey and went into a stable near the inn.

That very night, Mary's baby was born. She named the baby Jesus, and laid him in a manger where the lambs and cattle fed.

While the baby slept, an angel appeared in the sky above Bethlehem. Shepherds, who were watching over their flocks, saw the angel and were very afraid.

But the angel said to them, "Fear not: for I bring news of great joy to the world. Today the Son of God is born. You will find him lying in a manger. Glory to God in the highest, and on earth peace and good will to all people, everywhere."

The shepherds were amazed. They decided that they should leave their sheep and try to find this baby that the angel had called the Son of God.

They found the baby Jesus with Mary and Joseph in the stable.

Now, far away to the east, a great star blazed in the sky. Three wise men saw this new star and understood that it meant a great king had been born. The wise men came on camels to the city of Jerusalem. They wanted to tell King Herod that a new king had been born, one who would be known as the king of all kings.

When Herod heard this news, he was not very happy. He wanted to be the *only* king. But Herod pretended to be happy and asked the wise men to find this great, new king and bring back news of him.

The star guided the three wise men to the young child, Jesus.

When they found Mary and Joseph and the baby, the wise men dropped to their knees and said, "Behold, the Son of God." Then they gave Mary and the baby precious gifts of gold, frankincense, and myrrh.

The next morning, they set out toward Jerusalem to tell King Herod where they had found Jesus.

During the night, God came to them in a dream and warned them not to return to Herod, for he might wish to harm the child. So, the wise men decided to return home by another road.

An angel also appeared before Joseph and warned him of the danger. The angel said, "Arise and take the newborn child and his mother as quickly as you can into Egypt." Right away Joseph helped Mary and the baby onto their donkey and they rode to Egypt where they would be safe.

Mary and Joseph and baby Jesus stayed in Egypt until King Herod died. Then they came back to Nazareth where Joseph worked as a carpenter. Jesus helped him there and grew up to be known far and wide as Jesus of Nazareth.

And every year on Christmas Day we celebrate the birthday of Jesus. People all over the world come together and remember that night so long ago when the angels sang to the shepherds, and a star appeared in the sky, and the Son of God was born.

JOY TO THE WORLD!